THE SECRET OF THE HIDDEN SCROLLS

BOOK EIGHT
MIRACLES BY THE SEA

BY M. J. THOMAS

For my son, Payton. I love you, and I am proud of you!

—M.J.T.

ISBN: 978-1-5460-3379-0

WorthyKids
Hachette Book Group
1290 Avenue of the Americas
New York, NY 10104

Text copyright © 2020 by M. J. Thomas
Art copyright © 2020 by Hachette Book Group, Inc.

WorthyKids is a registered trademark of Hachette Book Group, Inc.

Library of Congress CIP data on file

Cover illustration by Graham Howells
Interior illustrations by Michelle Simpson
Designed by Georgina Chidlow-Irvin

Lexile® level 460L

Printed and bound in the U.S.A.
LSC-C
10 9 8 7 6 5 4 3 2 1

CONTENTS

PROLOGUE

Nine-year-old Peter and his ten-year-old sister, Mary, stood at the door to the huge, old house and waved as their parents drove away. Peter and Mary and their dog, Hank, would be spending the month with Great-Uncle Solomon.

Peter thought it would be the most boring month ever—until he realized Great-Uncle Solomon was an archaeologist. Great-Uncle Solomon showed them artifacts and treasures and told them stories about his travels around the globe. And then he shared his most amazing discovery of all—the Legend of the Hidden Scrolls! These weren't just dusty old scrolls. They held secrets—and they would lead to travel through time.

Soon Peter, Mary, and Hank were flung back in time to important moments in the Bible. They witnessed the Creation of the earth and helped Noah load the ark. They endured the plagues in Egypt and stood on top of the walls of Jericho. They watched David battle Goliath and faced lions with Daniel. They met the newborn King, Jesus. They had exciting adventures, all while trying to solve the secrets in the scrolls.

Now Peter and Mary are ready for their next adventure . . . as soon as they hear the lion's roar.

The Legend of the Hidden Scrolls
THE SCROLLS CONTAIN THE TRUTH YOU SEEK.
BREAK THE SEAL. UNROLL THE SCROLL.
AND YOU WILL SEE THE PAST UNFOLD.
AMAZING ADVENTURES ARE IN STORE
FOR THOSE WHO FOLLOW THE LION'S ROAR!

1

HEADS OR TAILS

Peter stared at the gold medallion in the palm of his hand. He rubbed his finger across the star imprinted on the large coin. It reminded him of his last adventure, when he and Mary had traveled back in time and met baby Jesus. He flipped the medallion in the air. He wondered when they would hear the lion's roar again and where they would go on their next adventure.

Peter caught the medallion and looked over at his older sister. "Hey, Mary," he said. "Heads or tails?"

Mary looked up from an old, dusty book. "I don't have time to play games. I'm reading."

Peter shrugged and turned to Great-Uncle Solomon. He was sitting in his leather chair reading a book too. Peter had no idea why Mary and Great-Uncle Solomon read so many big, boring books. "Hey, Great-Uncle Solomon!" he said. "Do you want to play heads or tails?"

Great-Uncle Solomon put his book down and adjusted his round glasses. "Sure! And speaking of tails . . . where's Hank?"

"I let him go outside to use the bathroom," said Peter. He put the medallion on his thumb. "Heads or tails? The side with the star is 'heads.'"

Great-Uncle Solomon leaned forward in his chair and rubbed his bushy white mustache. "Heads!"

Peter flicked the gold medallion high in the air.

"Be careful," Mary said. "Don't drop it."

4

Peter rolled his eyes. "I won't."

But he did. The medallion slipped through his fingers and rolled across the wood floor straight toward the front door.

"I warned you," said Mary, turning the page of her book.

"I've got it!" said Peter, chasing the medallion across the floor.

Bang! Bang!

Peter skidded to a stop and looked up at the tall wooden door. "Are you expecting visitors?"

Great-Uncle Solomon checked his pocket watch. "No," he said. "Your parents aren't supposed to be back from Africa for a couple more days."

Bang! Bang!

Mary tossed her book on the floor. "Maybe they're early!" She ran past Peter and swung the door wide open. Her shoulders slumped. "It's just Hank."

Bang! Bang! Hank couldn't get through the door because he had a long piece of rotten wood in his mouth.

Peter knelt in front of Hank. "What did you find?"

Hank dropped the wood on the ground and wagged his tail. Peter picked it up and turned it so it could fit through the door. It was taller than Peter and had a paddle on one end.

"It's an ancient oar," said Great-Uncle Solomon. "Hank must have gone into the barn."

Now Mary looked interested. "You have a barn?"

"You never noticed the barn?" said Peter. "You really need to get outside more."

"Yes," said Great-Uncle Solomon. "I keep some of my bigger archaeological discoveries in the barn."

Mary's eyes got as big as the gold medallion. "Can we see?"

"Of course," said Great-Uncle Solomon. "I want to show you something I've been working on. Follow me."

Peter picked up the medallion and set it on a

bookshelf. Then he grabbed his leather adventure bag and followed Mary out of the house.

Great-Uncle Solomon led the way around the huge house made of brick and stone. Peter looked at the green ivy crawling up the walls to the second floor.

They finally made it to the back of the house. Peter noticed a small tower circled in windows on the back corner of the house. "What's up there?" he said.

"I'll show you later," said Great-Uncle Solomon.

"Woof!" Hank barked and ran toward the big red barn. He disappeared into the barn.

Great-Uncle Solomon slid the door open, and Peter walked in. Hank was running in circles, sniffing everything. Peter walked in and took a look around. Hay bales were stacked in corners, and the shelves were covered in all kinds of tools and supplies.

Mary picked a first-aid kit off a shelf and turned to Peter. "This might be helpful on our next adventure. Who knows what might happen?"

"Good idea," said Great-Uncle Solomon. "Put it in your adventure bag."

Peter slipped the kit into the bag. He picked up a hammer and a box of nails from a shelf, swung the hammer hard, and whacked a nail into a piece of wood.

"You're pretty good with a hammer," said Great-Uncle Solomon.

"I had a lot of practice helping Noah on the ark," he said.

"What did you want to show us?" interrupted Mary.

"I almost forgot," said Great-Uncle Solomon. "It's right over here." He walked toward a long canvas tarp. "Help me pull this off."

Peter and Mary each grabbed a corner of the tarp and pulled at the same time.

"Here it is!" said Great-Uncle Solomon.

All it looked like to Peter was a bunch of rotten wood piled on the floor. "What is it?"

Mary rubbed her chin. "Is it a boat?"

"Yes," said Great-Uncle Solomon. "You're right!"

Of course she was right—she was always right. Peter thought it looked more like the skeleton of a boat. "I knew what it was," he said. "I just wanted to see if you did."

"Sure, you did," Mary said. "Where did you discover it, Great-Uncle Solomon?"

"I found it buried in mud beside the Sea of Galilee in Israel," said Great-Uncle Solomon. "I believe it belonged to a very important person!"

"Who?" asked Peter.

Roar!

The lion's roar came from the house and echoed through the barn.

"I'll have to tell you when you get back from your adventure," said Great-Uncle Solomon. "Hurry!"

Roar!

"Let's go, Mary!" Peter ran out of the barn with Mary and Hank. They raced around the house, through the front door, past the suit of armor, and slid to a stop in front of the tall library doors. Peter reached for the handle shaped like a lion's head. He turned it.

Click!

Peter swung the door open.

Roar! The sound came from behind the tall bookshelves on the right. Mary quickly found the red book with the lion's head painted in gold on the cover. She pulled it off the shelf. Peter watched the bookshelf slide open to reveal the hidden room. It was dark, except for a glowing clay pot in the center of the room that held the Hidden Scrolls.

Peter ran over and pulled out a scroll. "Let's open this one."

"What's on the red wax seal?" said Mary.

"It looks like a heart," said Peter.

"Let's see where the scroll takes us!" said Mary.

Peter broke the red wax seal on the scroll.

The walls shook. The floor rumbled. Books fell to the floor. The library crumbled around them and disappeared. Then everything was dark and quiet.

2

So Many Scrolls

Peter squinted. "It's so dark!"

"*Shhhh*, don't be so loud," whispered Mary. "Someone might hear us."

"Where are we?" asked Peter.

"I don't know," said Mary. "Did you bring a flashlight?"

"Oh yeah," said Peter. "I almost forgot." He reached into the leather bag and pulled out the flashlight. He slowly moved the light around. They were standing in a large room with white marble floors. There were tall pillars all around,

 and light reflected off gold-covered walls.

"This is amazing!" said Mary.

Peter aimed the flashlight at a tall candle stand with seven branches. "Look! It's a menorah! Just like the one we saw in the Tabernacle in the desert."

Hank ran over and sniffed the menorah. Then he darted to the left.

Peter followed Hank with the flashlight. "Wow!" A tall curtain stretched across one side of the room. It was red, blue, and purple and decorated with large golden angels.

Mary snapped her fingers. "We must be in the Temple in Jerusalem."

"*Grrrr!*"

Peter turned to Hank. He was growling at something across the room.

"We must not be alone," said Mary.

Peter saw a glow coming from a hallway. His heart pounded as he shined the flashlight around the room. He found a door to their right. "Hurry," he whispered. "Let's hide in there."

They ran across the marble floor into the room. Peter shut the door behind them and turned around. The room was full of tables and shelves and scrolls—lots of scrolls.

"Look at all these scrolls," said Mary.

"There must be thousands of them," said Peter.

"I think we're in an ancient library," Mary said.

Hank growled at the door.

Mary pointed at a table covered in scrolls. "Let's hide over there."

Peter, Mary, and Hank crawled under the table.

The door swung open.

"Don't move," whispered Peter.

A large man wearing armor walked into the library. *He must be a temple guard*, thought Peter. The man held a torch in one hand and a sword in the other. He held up the torch and peered around the room. He walked closer to their hiding place.

"Woof!" barked Hank.

"Who's there?" shouted the guard. He ducked and held the torch under the table.

Hank growled louder.

"What are you kids doing under there?" said the guard.

"We thought we would do a little reading," said Peter as he climbed out.

The guard narrowed his eyes. "How did you get in here?"

"We can't tell you," said Mary.

"You need to take your dog and get out," said the guard.

"Yes, sir," said Peter. They headed for the door.

"STOP!"

Peter, Mary, and Hank froze.

"What's in your hand?" asked the guard.

"A bag."

"No." He pointed at Mary. "What's in *her* hand?"

"A scroll," said Mary.

"You're stealing!" said the guard. He raised his sword.

"We aren't stealing," said Peter. "It's ours."

The guard grabbed the scroll out of Mary's hand. "You are under arrest."

"*Grrrr!*" Hank ran at the guard.

"Stay back!" The guard swung his torch. Hank jumped over it and ran in a circle around the guard. The guard spun around. Hank leaped and grabbed the scroll out of his hand.

"Run, Hank!" shouted Peter.

Hank took off like a lightning bolt. He ran through the guard's legs, under the tables, and out the door.

"Don't stop!" shouted Mary. "We'll find you!"

The guard pointed his sword at Peter and Mary. "You aren't going anywhere."

"We should have brought weapons," Mary whispered.

"You don't need weapons, remember?" said Peter.

"You're right," said Mary.

"I think it's time for a karate lesson," said Peter.

Mary leapt into the air, did a spinning kick, and knocked the sword from the guard's hand.

Peter ran over and picked up the sword. His arm shook as he pointed the heavy weapon at the guard.

"Help!" shouted the guard.

"Let's get out of here!" said Peter.

Peter dropped the sword and ran out of the library with Mary right behind. They ran out of the Temple and across the huge dark room, down

a hallway, and through a door. Moonlight shined down on the courtyard. Peter stopped and looked back at the tall white building with white marble pillars and a golden roof.

"We are definitely at the Temple in Jerusalem," said Mary. "The guard must have been protecting the Sacred Scrolls of the Bible."

"No wonder he wanted *our* scroll so much," said Peter.

"There they are!" The guard's shout echoed across the courtyard. This time he wasn't alone. A large group of guards followed him as he ran toward Peter and Mary.

Mary pointed at a staircase on the other side of the courtyard. "Let's go down those stairs!"

Peter and Mary ran toward the stairs. There was a tall iron gate at the bottom. Peter raced down and pushed against the gate with all his might.

"It won't budge!" said Peter. "We're trapped!"

3

Into the Desert

Mary pushed too, but it was no use. Peter looked over his shoulder. The guards were at the top of the steps. Peter felt a strong gust of wind blow past him.

Whoosh. The gate flew open.

"Come on," said Mary. "They're right behind us!" Peter followed her as she ran through the gate.

Clank! The gate swung shut and trapped the temple guards inside the tall walls.

"Who closed the gate?" asked Mary.

Peter looked around. "I don't know."

"Let's keep moving," said Mary. "We've got to find Hank."

"We would love to stay and chat," said Peter as he turned to leave. "But we have places to go and people to see."

"This isn't over!" the guard shouted. "We will find you, and we will get that scroll!"

Peter and Mary ran toward the nearest road. They raced farther and farther into the moonlit city. Peter saw rows of clay and brick houses. Smaller roads and paths led to even more houses and shops. It was getting hard to catch his breath.

"Hank!" shouted Peter.

"Not so loud," said Mary. "You're going to wake up the whole city."

Suddenly, a voice echoed out of the darkness. "Come this way."

Peter skidded to a stop. The voice had come from a dark path on their left.

"What do we do?" whispered Mary. "What if it's a guard?"

"Don't be afraid," said the voice.

"Wait, I recognize that voice," said Peter.

He led the way down the dark path and turned the corner. Peter saw Michael the angel smiling at him. Hank was sitting next to Michael, holding the scroll in his mouth.

"Good boy," said Peter as he took the scroll from Hank.

"You two got into trouble quickly," said Michael.

"Where have you been?" said Peter. "We were almost

captured by a bunch of temple guards with swords!"

"Who do you think opened the gate?" said Michael.

"But I didn't see you," said Peter.

Michael nodded. "I didn't want the guards to see me."

"I knew it was you!" said Mary.

Peter rolled his eyes. "Of course you did."

"It's good to see you again," said Michael. "It's been a while."

"How long? What year is this?" asked Mary.

"You're going to have to figure that out on your own," said Michael. "But right now, we need to get out of Jerusalem before the guards find you."

Peter, Mary, and Hank followed Michael to the city wall and through an opening. A desert stretched before them in all directions.

"The desert is a great place to hide," said Michael. "There aren't many people, and there is a safe cave where we can talk."

They walked and walked across the rough sand under the bright moon.

"How much farther?" asked Peter. "My legs are starting to get tired."

Michael pointed to a hill in front of them. "We're almost there," he said. "The cave is in that hill."

Peter and Mary followed Michael up the hill and walked into the mouth of the cave.

"We should be safe in here," said Michael.

"Now, it's time to go over the rules of your adventure." He held up one finger. "First rule: You have to solve the secret in the scroll in seven days or you will be stuck here."

Mary nodded. "We definitely have to solve it. We have to get back before our parents come home."

Michael held up two fingers. "Second rule: You can't tell anyone where you are from or that you are from the future."

"We won't," said Peter.

Michael held up three fingers. "Third rule: You can't try to change the past. Now let's take a look at that scroll."

Peter unrolled the scroll. There were four words written in strange letters on it.

"What language is this?" asked Peter.

Mary peeked over his shoulder. "It's Greek."

Peter shrugged. "It's all Greek to me."

"Too bad Dad's not here," said Mary. "He knows Greek much better than I do."

Peter thought about his parents. He missed them so much. He couldn't wait to see them and tell them all about the amazing adventures he'd had.

"You need to get away from Jerusalem," said Michael. "The temple guards will keep looking for you."

Michael looked out of the cave. "You also need to be on guard for the enemy—Satan."

Peter joined Michael and watched the sun begin to rise behind the Temple's golden roof. The desert sand sparkled in the morning light.

"God is building his Kingdom," said Michael. "And Satan will do everything he can to destroy God's Kingdom and the King so he can try to rule this world."

"Where should we go?" asked Mary.

"Do you have a map?" said Michael.

"Oh yeah!" said Peter. "I think I still have the map from our last adventure." He dug deep in his leather bag and pulled out the map of Israel. He unrolled it and showed it to Michael.

Michael ran his finger along the map. "You need to go north along the Jordan River to the Sea of Galilee. And you need to make it before the sun sets."

"That looks like a long way," said Mary.

Peter's shoulders slumped. "It might not be hard for you to fly that far," he said to Michael. "But it will take us forever to walk that far."

"That's true. We'll never make it in time," said Mary.

"Don't worry," said Michael. "Follow me."

They walked out of the cave. Michael pulled a trumpet out of his robe and blew it. The sound filled the desert. Two white horses ran over a hill. They were big, beautiful, and fast. They

both wore saddles and
had bags hanging from
their sides.

"These are special
horses," said Michael.
"They will take you
where you need to
go. The saddle bags
have food and water in
them for your journey."

"What do we do when we get to the Sea of
Galilee?" asked Mary.

"You will find a boat on the shore," said
Michael.

"Then what do we do?" asked Peter.

"Just trust God. He will take you where you
need to go." Michael spread his mighty wings.
"Now go, before the guards find you!" Then he
flew into the bright sky.

4

WELCOME TO GALILEE

The white horses carried Peter, Mary, and Hank across the hot desert. They were fast—really fast. Peter kept a tight grip on the reins.

They journeyed north beside the Jordan River all day—stopping only once to eat some of the food Michael had given them.

"How much farther?" asked Peter.

Mary pointed ahead. "Is that the sea?"

Peter squinted. "I think so!"

The sun set as the horses came to a stop at the shore of the Sea of Galilee.

"We made it!" said Mary.

Peter hopped off his horse and rubbed his back side. "I'm so sore!" he groaned. "And tired!"

"Now what?" said Mary, hopping off her horse.

"I guess we find the boat Michael told us about," said Peter.

"Woof!" Hank barked as he ran along the shore. Peter and Mary followed behind him.

They found a large wooden boat docked on the shore. It had a tall mast and a white sail. Peter thought it looked like a pirate ship, but not quite as big.

Hank jumped into the boat. Peter helped Mary in, then climbed in behind her. He tossed the adventure bag on top of some mats at the back of the boat.

Peter looked around for oars but didn't find

any. He looked over the bow of the boat at the dark water and waited for something to happen. Hank barked at fish swimming by.

"What are we supposed to do now?" said Peter.

"I guess we wait for God," said Mary.

The scroll started shaking in the adventure bag. Peter ran to the bag, pulled out the scroll, and unrolled it. The first word glowed, and the Greek letters twisted into the word: GOD.

"We solved the first word of the secret!" shouted Peter.

Mary put her hands on her hips. "Well, actually I did."

"I guess so," said Peter. "If you want to be picky about it."

Hank howled at something in the night sky.

"What is it, Hank?" said Peter.

The trees along the shore began to sway. A strong gust of wind filled the sail. The boat jolted forward and sent Peter and Mary tumbling into Hank as it pulled away from the shore. The wind pushed the boat swiftly through the water.

Peter leaned over the side and watched the waves splash against the boat. The moon's glow reflected across the Sea of Galilee. "Mary, come look at this."

Peter looked back over his shoulder. Mary and Hank were sound asleep on the mats.

Peter walked back and sat down next to them. He pulled out his adventure journal and drew a picture of the boat. Then he wrote:

Day 1
The boat is awesome. I love being on the sea. The water is pretty at night, and I can see the lights of the towns along the shore. I can't wait to see where God is taking us, but I hope the guards don't find us.

Peter put the journal away and stared at the stars as he drifted off to sleep.

Peter woke the next morning with the sun in his eyes. He stood up and walked to the front of the boat. It was still moving quickly across the water. Mary stretched and rubbed her eyes.

"Where do you think we're going?" asked Peter.

"I don't know," said Mary. "We'll have to trust God. He's gotten us this far."

Peter felt the wind at his back as he looked out over the water. "It looks like we're headed to shore!"

The wind blew harder, and the boat moved faster. Hank barked at something on the shore.

Peter squinted. The shore was getting closer. He saw boats and a young man with a dark, curly beard cleaning fishing nets. "How do we stop this thing?"

Mary looked around the boat. "I'm not sure!"

"Well, we better figure it out, because we're about to crash!"

The young man dropped the nets and started wildly waving his arms.

"Slow down!" the man shouted. "You're going too fast!"

Peter's heart raced. The other boats were getting closer. "We don't know how to stop!"

The young man stepped into the water. "Lower the sail!"

Peter and Mary untied the ropes and pulled down the billowing sail. The boat quickly slowed. Peter thought it felt like someone had pushed the brakes.

They barely missed hitting the other boat, and finally skidded to a stop on the sandy shore.

The young man wiped sweat from his brow. "That was close!"

"Sorry," said Peter. "We're new at this."

"Welcome to Capernaum," said the young

man. "My name is Simon Peter, but you can call me Simon."

Peter grabbed the adventure bag and hopped out of the boat. "My name is Peter too!"

"It's a good name," said Simon. "It means 'rock' . . . you must be very strong."

Peter liked Simon right away.

Hank and Mary jumped out of the boat. Hank wagged his tail.

"This is Hank," said Peter. "And this is my sister, Mary."

"It is nice to meet you, Mary," said Simon.

Hank ran over and sniffed the fishing nets.

"You're not going to find any fish," Simon said. "I didn't have a very good morning at sea."

"Are you a fisherman?" asked Peter.

"I used to be," Simon said. "Until I met my new friend!"

"What do you mean?" said Mary.

Simon tossed the nets into his boat. "My friend asked me to stop fishing and follow him instead." Simon smiled. "You have to meet him! Follow me."

They made their way up the shore and headed into the small village. They walked along a dirt path lined by small shops selling fish, bread, and cheese. Peter wanted to stop and eat, but he could tell Simon was in a hurry.

"You're going to love him!" said Simon.

They turned the corner and Peter saw a crowd of people trying to get into a small stone house.

"Your friend must be very popular," said Mary.

"People come from all over to see him," said Simon. "Everywhere he goes, the crowds seem to get bigger and bigger."

Peter stopped as four men carrying a man on a mat hustled past them toward the door. They couldn't get in. It was too crowded.

Then Peter noticed some older, important looking men wearing dark robes.

"Move out of the way!" said one of the men wearing black from head to toe. He pushed people aside with a tall golden staff.

"How rude!" said Mary.

"Who are those guys?" said Peter.

"They're Pharisees," said Simon. "They're religious leaders who think they are better than everyone else, and that God only likes them. They don't like my friend—or anyone else!"

"Everyone go away!" shouted the Pharisee with the golden staff. "There's no room for any more of you people!" Then he turned and shoved his way into the house with the rest of the Pharisees.

"We have to get in there!" said one of the men carrying the mat. "He's the only one who can help!"

Peter turned to Simon. "Who is your friend?"

"His name is—" Simon started to say.

"Woof! Woof!" Hank barked and ran between people's legs into the house.

"We'll be right back," said Peter. "We have to get Hank."

5

THE CEILING IS FALLING!

Peter and Mary squeezed through the crowd and made it through the front door of the house. The room was crowded—but it was really quiet. Everyone was listening to a man standing in the middle of the room.

"Look," said Peter. "There's Hank sitting in front of that man."

"Let's get him," said Mary as they slipped through the listeners.

"God has sent me to give you good news! The Kingdom of God is here," said the man. "To enter the Kingdom, you must have faith like a child." He stopped speaking and looked right at Peter and Mary. "Like these two children right here."

"Sorry," said Peter. "We didn't mean to interrupt."

"You are welcome here," said the man. "Children are always welcome."

He smiled at them and started talking to the people again.

"There's something familiar about him," Mary whispered to Peter.

Peter looked into the man's eyes. He had seen those eyes before—in a manger in Bethlehem. A warm feeling of joy, peace, and love filled Peter's body. "It's Jesus!"

Peter and Mary sat in front of Jesus and listened.

"Ouch!" Peter looked up at the ceiling. "Something hit me on the head."

"Ouch!" Mary rubbed her head. "Me too."

"It's coming from up there," said Peter. "Let's get out of the way."

Peter, Mary, and Hank moved to the side of the room where the Pharisees were.

"*Grrrr!*" Hank growled at them.

Peter stared at the golden staff one Pharisee was holding. The Pharisee slammed the staff on the ground in front of Hank. "Keep that mangy mutt away from me!" he snarled.

"Sorry," said Peter. "He likes most people."

"Pharisees are not *most* people," said the man.

"We are God's special people," said another Pharisee. "We know more about God than all of the lowly people in here."

"We know about God too," said Mary.

The man with the staff laughed. Then the others joined in.

"What's so funny?" said Peter.

The man leaned against his staff and stared down at Peter. "You don't know anything about God," he said. "You are just silly little children."

"I'm not little, and she is very smart," said Peter. "Go ahead, ask her any question."

The Pharisee rolled his eyes. "We're not here to play childish games," he said.

"Why *are* you here?" asked Mary.

"You children have so many questions. We're here to find out more about this troublemaker."

The Pharisee pointed at Jesus. "Now leave me alone. I'm busy."

Hank barked at something above Peter. Peter looked up and saw a big hole in the ceiling. Then a man stuck his head through the hole.

"There's Jesus," said the man to his friends. "Keep digging!" Parts of the ceiling rained down into the room. "The hole is big enough," said the first man. "Lower him down."

Peter watched them lower the man on the mat through the hole in and set him on the ground right in front of Jesus.

"Teacher, our friend is paralyzed," said one of the men. "Please heal him."

A hush fell over the room.

Jesus looked up through the hole at the man's friends and smiled.

Then he leaned down beside the paralyzed man. "My child," said Jesus. "Your sins are forgiven."

"What did he say?" said the Pharisee with the golden staff.

"He said the man's sins are forgiven," said Peter.

"Quiet!" said the Pharisee. "I heard what he said. I just can't believe he said it."

"Why?" asked Mary.

"It's blasphemy!" said the Pharisee.

"What's blasphemy?" asked Peter.

"Blasphemy is a lie against God," said another Pharisee. "Only God can forgive sins."

Jesus stood up and looked across the room at the Pharisees.

"Why do you question in your hearts what I have said?" asked Jesus. "Would it be easier for me to forgive his sins or to heal his body?"

The Pharisees looked at each other. "How did

he know what we were thinking?" whispered one of them.

"I will prove that I have the power to forgive sins," said Jesus.

The crowd grew completely silent. The paralyzed man's friends poked their heads through the hole in the roof.

Jesus walked closer to the paralyzed man. "Stand up!"

Peter held his breath. The man stood up. Then he jumped and ran around the crowded room. The people cheered!

"It's a miracle!" shouted his friends through the hole in the roof. "Praise God!"

"This is the most amazing thing I have ever seen!" said a woman in the crowd.

The room buzzed with excitement. But Peter could tell not everyone was happy.

"This is not good!" said the Pharisee with the

staff to his friend. "It's almost like Jesus cares about these worthless people."

"He claims to do these amazing things in God's name," said another Pharisee.

"Jesus can't be from God, because he's not one of us," said another.

"We must stop him," said the Pharisee with the golden staff. "Or soon everyone will be listening to him instead of us."

Peter nudged Mary. He pointed across the room. Several temple guards had come in the door and were rushing toward the Pharisees.

"Let's get out of here," whispered Mary.

Peter, Mary, and Hank slowly weaved their way to the door.

"Excuse me, sir!" said a temple guard. "We have a problem."

"What's the problem?" said the Pharisee with the golden staff.

"One of the sacred scrolls was stolen!" said the guard.

"You had one job!" shouted the Pharisee. "How did you let this happen?"

"I'm not sure how the thieves got in," said the guard.

"How many men were there?" asked another Pharisee.

"There were no men," answered the temple guard. "Just two children and a dog."

"Is this a joke?" asked the Pharisee with the staff.

"No, sir," said the guard.

"Well, have you found them?" asked the Pharisee.

"No," answered the guard. "They escaped into the desert."

"Well then, I think I found them," said the Pharisee. "Are those the children you're looking for?"

Peter had just reached the front door. He spun around and saw the Pharisee pointing right at him.

"That's them!" shouted the guard.

"Capture those thieves!" said the Pharisee with the golden staff.

6

A WILD RIDE

"Run!" shouted Peter.

Hank bolted out the door. Peter and Mary darted and dodged through the crowd right behind him.

"Where's Hank going?" shouted Mary.

"I don't know!" said Peter. "Just keep following him."

Hank ran to the shore and stopped beside their boat.

Peter looked over his shoulder. The temple guards weren't far behind. "Hurry, get in the boat!"

Hank jumped into the boat. Mary climbed in next. Peter grunted and pushed the boat off the shore and into the sea.

Mary grabbed the rope and pulled up the sail. "Throw the bag to me!"

Peter tossed the bag as hard as he could, but it fell into the water.

"Mary! Why didn't you catch it?"

"You didn't throw it far enough," said Mary.

"I hope the water doesn't ruin everything in the bag," said Peter.

He waded into the water. A strong wind filled the boat's sail. The wood creaked and the boat floated farther away from him.

"Stop!" shouted a guard. "Don't move!"

Peter looked at the guards. Then he looked at the leather bag floating in the water.

"Hurry!" shouted Mary. "The wind is pushing us away."

Peter looked back at the guard once more. Then he dove into the water and swam toward the bag as fast as he could. He grabbed it and slung it over his shoulder.

"Faster!" shouted Mary.

Peter pushed through the murky water. He finally caught up with the boat.

"Throw the bag," said Mary.

Peter used all of his strength and threw the bag in the air. This time Mary caught it.

"Get in!" said Mary. "The guards just found a boat!"

Peter grabbed on to the side of the boat. He tried to pull himself in, but the sides were too high and his arms were too tired.

"I'll help you! Hold on," said Mary. But just then, the wind blew harder. The sail filled, and the boat raced across the water. Peter held on tightly, but his fingers started to cramp.

"Don't let go!" said Mary. "We're getting away."

Peter couldn't hold on any longer. He let go and fell back into the water. He tried to swim to the boat, but it was moving too fast.

"Keep rowing!" shouted a guard. "We almost have them."

Mary threw a fishing net toward Peter. "Grab the net! I'll pull you in."

Peter used his last bit of energy to grab the net. The wind blew harder, and Peter and the boat sped through the water.

"Just hold on," said Mary. "We're going too fast for me to pull you in."

The ride through the water was rough. Peter bounced and spun, but he didn't let go.

"Ouch!" shouted Peter. "Something just hit my leg."

"Don't let go," said Mary. "We've almost lost them."

The boat raced through the water. Peter held onto the net for dear life. The temple guards were nowhere to be seen. Suddenly, the wind stopped blowing, and the boat slowed to a stop.

"My leg is killing me!" groaned Peter. "Pull me in."

Mary pulled the net as hard as she could, and Peter slowly moved closer to the boat.

He felt a throbbing pain in his right leg. Peter looked down and saw the water turning red. "My leg is bleeding," he said.

"Did you know that blood attracts sharks?" asked Mary.

"Why did you have to remind me?" said Peter. "Get me out of here."

"Don't worry," said Mary. "I don't think there are any sharks in the Sea of Galilee."

"Easy for you to say," said Peter. "I don't want to find out."

"Did you know the Sea of Galilee isn't actually a sea?" said Mary. "It's a huge lake."

"We can talk about it later," said Peter. "Just get me out of the water!"

Mary kept pulling the net. "Hank, help!" she said.

Hank grabbed onto the net with his teeth and pulled. Peter started moving faster.

"Good job, Hank," said Mary.

Mary and Hank dragged the fishing net into the boat, but Peter wasn't the only thing in the net. It was full of slimy, floppy fish.

"Yuck!" said Mary. "You stink!"

"It's not me," said Peter. "It's all these fish."

"If you say so," said Mary.

"Get me out of this net," said Peter. "I'm stuck."

Mary tried to untangle him from the net, but it only got worse.

"Wait," said Peter. "I think there's a pocket knife in the bag."

Mary opened the bag and pulled out the knife. She started cutting the net. Peter and the fish spilled out onto the boat deck.

"Freedom!" shouted Peter.

"That's a big cut on your leg," said Mary.

Peter looked down at the blood flowing from a huge gash in his leg. Suddenly he felt weak and dizzy.

"I know what to do," said Mary. She pulled the first-aid kit out of the bag. She rubbed an alcohol swab on Peter's cut.

"Ouch!" shouted Peter. "That stings!"

"Well, you don't want to get an infection, do you?" said Mary. She put a bandage on the cut.

"How did you know what to do?" asked Peter.

"I read about it in a book—*My First First-Aid Kit: A Kid's Survival Guide*," said Mary.

Peter stood up and slowly limped around. "It feels a little better."

Mary put the first-aid kit back in the bag.

Peter's stomach growled. "All that swimming made me hungry." He picked up one of the slimy fish. "How about fish for dinner?"

"How are we going to cook it?" asked Mary.

"I don't know," said Peter. "Maybe we can have sushi."

Mary wrinkled her nose. "I don't like sushi."

Peter hobbled to the front of the boat. They were approaching land. He spotted smoke coming from the beach.

As the boat floated closer to shore, he saw a large group of men sitting around a fire. "Maybe they will help us cook the fish," he said.

Mary joined Peter at the front of the boat. "They could be temple guards."

"I didn't think about that," Peter said. "Duck, so they don't see us."

They dove under the stinky fishing nets. Peter felt the bottom of the boat scrape against the shore.

"*Grrrr!*" Hank growled next to them.

Peter heard footsteps coming across the sand. *Crunch. Crunch.*

His heart pounded in his chest. "Keep quiet," he whispered.

7

Dining with Disciples

The footsteps stopped.

"It looks empty," said a deep voice.

"I'll take a look inside," said another voice.

Peter felt the boat move a little. Someone landed on his leg—his hurt leg.

"Ouch!" Peter shouted.

Someone pulled the fishing nets away. Peter saw a tall man holding a torch.

Hank wagged his tail. It was Simon.

"There you are," said Simon. "I wondered where you all ran off to."

"We were running from the temple guards," said Peter.

"Why were temple guards chasing you?" said Simon.

Mary gave Peter *the look*. "Um, we can't tell you," she said.

"That's okay," said Simon. "You can keep your secrets for now."

A couple of other men walked up and looked in the boat.

"Let me introduce you to some more of Jesus' friends," said Simon. "This is James and his brother, John."

"Are you fishermen?" asked James.

"Not exactly," said Mary.

Simon pointed at all the fish in the boat. "You made a pretty good catch."

James laughed. "They're better at fishing than you are, Simon."

John laughed too. "Yeah, Simon didn't catch anything today."

Peter's stomach growled. "Can you help us cook the fish? There's plenty for everyone."

"Sure!" said Simon. He rubbed his belly. "I'm pretty hungry myself."

"Join us at our camp. We'll have a feast," said James.

Peter grabbed the adventure bag and climbed out of the boat. "Sounds good to me!"

Everyone grabbed some fish except Mary. She said she didn't like how slimy they were.

"Is Jesus with you?" Mary asked the men.

"Yes," said Simon. "He went to pray, but he should be back soon."

Simon used the torch to light the way. They walked up the shore to the campfire. There were several young men warming themselves around the fire.

"Hey, Simon!" said one of the men. "You finally caught some fish!"

"Not exactly," said Simon. "Our young friends, Peter and Mary, caught the fish, and they're going to share with us."

"Thanks," said one of the men. "Simon's not the best fisherman."

"Ha, ha, very funny," said Simon. "This is my brother, Andrew. As you can see, I got all the good looks in the family."

Peter laughed and his stomach rumbled. Something smelled delicious.

"The three guys baking bread are Philip, Bartholomew, and the other James," said Simon. "The guys over there fixing the fishing nets are Thomas, Matthew, Thaddeus, and the other Simon." The men waved as they were introduced. Simon looked around. "We're missing someone."

"Grrrr!" Hank growled at something at the edge of the camp.

A man walked out of the shadows.

"There you are," said Simon. "Were you off counting the money again?"

The man stared at Peter and Mary with suspicious eyes. "Something like that," he grunted.

"This is Judas Iscariot," said Simon.

"What's in the bag you're carrying?" asked Judas.

Peter held the bag tight. "It's nothing."

"*Grrrr!*" Hank stood in front of Peter and growled at Judas.

As Judas backed away, Simon said, "Hank doesn't seem to like you, Judas."

"Has anyone seen Jesus?" asked Simon.

"He's still up the mountain praying," said Andrew.

"Well, that could take a while," said Simon. "Let's go ahead and eat."

The disciples cooked the fish and handed out the warm bread. Peter thought it was the best thing he had ever tasted. Peter, Mary, and Hank ate more fish and bread than they had ever eaten in their lives. While they ate, the disciples took turns telling about what they used to do before they met Jesus. They all agreed that following Jesus was worth leaving their old lives behind.

There was so much food that even Peter couldn't finish it all. He wrapped up some fish and bread and put it in the adventure bag for later.

"When do you think Jesus will be back?" asked Mary.

"He might be gone all night," said Simon. "Sometimes he prays until the morning."

Mary yawned. "I'm getting tired."

Peter rubbed the bandage on his leg. He winced. "My leg is really hurting!"

"What happened?" asked Simon.

"A little boating accident," said Peter. "I'm sure it will be okay in the morning."

"Do you have someplace to sleep?" asked Simon.

"In our boat," said Peter as he hobbled back toward the shore.

"Well, we'll see you in the morning," said Simon.

Peter, Mary, and Hank climbed into the boat and laid down on their mats. Peter stared into the starry night sky. The waves slowly rocked the boat.

"We're going to see Jesus tomorrow," said Mary.

"I can't wait," said Peter, and drifted off to sleep.

8

THE GREAT HEALER

"Wake up!" shouted Simon.

Peter stood up and rubbed his eyes. He saw Simon and Andrew climbing into a fishing boat.

"*Woof!* barked Hank. He ran to the front of the boat. Mary yawned and followed him.

"Are you going fishing?" asked Peter.

"No," answered Simon. "We are getting the boat ready for Jesus."

"Here he comes," said Andrew.

Peter looked at the shore. Jesus was walking toward Simon's boat. As he climbed on board, he caught Peter's eye and smiled. Simon pulled up the sail, and they were off.

"Where are you going?" shouted Peter.

"To Bethsaida!" said Simon.

"Where's that?" said Peter.

"Follow me!" said Jesus as he waved to them.

Peter felt the wind blow. It filled the sail, and the boat started moving through the water behind Simon's boat.

"Here we go!" said Peter.

Hank stuck his head over the side of the boat. The wind blew through his fur.

"How far away is Bethsaida?" asked Peter.

Mary took the map out of the adventure bag and unrolled it.

"It doesn't look too far. It might be about ten miles away."

"I hope it doesn't take too long to get there. My leg really hurts!"

"Let's see what the cut looks like," said Mary.

Peter peeled back the bandage. "Ouch!"

"Oh no!" said Mary. "It looks infected."

"I think it's getting worse," said Peter. "I hope we can solve the secret of the scroll and get home so I can go to the doctor."

"Me too," said Mary. "We only have four days left to solve it, or we'll be stuck here."

Peter slowly limped over to the bag and took out the scroll. He unrolled it and read, "GOD _____ _____ _____."

"*Woof! Woof!*" Hank ran to the front of the boat and looked up. A ball of light streaked through the blue sky. It was coming straight toward the boat.

"Watch out!" shouted Peter. He ran to the back of the boat with Mary.

The ball of light grew bigger as it got closer to the boat. Suddenly, Peter saw wings coming out of the light, and Michael landed on the boat. Sparks flew as he skidded to a stop.

"Michael!" said Mary. "Why are you in such a hurry?"

Peter glanced at the fishing boat. Jesus and the others were talking and sailing like nothing had happened.

"Don't worry. They did not see me," said Michael. "I don't have much time, but I wanted to see how you two are doing."

"Not too good," said Mary. "We've only solved one word on the scroll, and Peter has a cut on his leg that's getting worse."

"Let me see," said Michael. Peter pulled back the bandage so the angel could take a look.

"That doesn't look good," said Michael.

"Can you help me?" asked Peter.

"No," said Michael. "But I know someone who can."

"Of course!" said Peter. He couldn't believe he hadn't thought of it before. "Jesus can help."

"That's true!" said Mary. "The Bible says Jesus is the Great Healer."

Just then the scroll started shaking. Mary grabbed the scroll and unrolled it. The third word glowed and twisted into the word: THE.

"We solved two words," said Peter. "GOD _____ THE _____."

"Actually, *I* solved them," said Mary.

"There is no time to argue," said Michael. "A large crowd has gathered to meet Jesus in Bethsaida. I believe Satan is going to try to cause trouble."

"Should we stay away?" asked Mary.

"No, you need to be there. Don't be afraid. Have faith in God."

"We will," said Peter.

"And don't forget to tell Jesus about your cut," said Michael. He spread his wings and shot into the air like a lightning bolt.

A few minutes later, both boats landed on the shore of Bethsaida. A large group of people was gathered. Peter saw old people and babies, people who looked healthy and people who looked really sick. Jesus and his friends climbed out and headed up a big hill. The crowd followed Jesus.

"Wait for us!" shouted Peter, but Simon didn't hear him.

Peter grabbed the bag and started limping up the hill with Mary and Hank.

He stopped and checked his leg. The cut was red and swollen. "It's getting worse! My whole body hurts. I don't think I can go any farther."

Hank leaned against him.

Mary grabbed Peter's arm and pulled him up. "We have to keep going," she said. "I'll help you."

They finally made it to the top of the hill. Peter saw Jesus talking to some people.

"I have to get to Jesus," said Peter as he stumbled through the crowd.

Judas Iscariot stepped in front of Peter. "Stop! I'm not letting any children see Jesus right now. He's too busy."

"Grrrr!" growled Hank.

"But I have to," said Peter. He saw Jesus walk up behind Judas.

"Do not stop them," said Jesus. "Let the children come to me."

"Follow me," said Jesus. They walked over to a small rock and sat down. "It is good to see you, Peter and Mary."

"Woof!" barked Hank.

Jesus bent down and pet Hank. "It's good to see you too, Hank."

"You know our names?" asked Peter.

"Of course I do," said Jesus. "I knew you before you were born. I have seen every step you've ever taken. I even saw you at the creation of the earth."

"You were there when the world was created?" asked Peter.

"Yes," said Jesus. "My Father and I created everything!"

Just then, the scroll started shaking in the adventure bag. Peter pulled it out and unrolled it. The fourth word glowed and transformed into the word: WORLD.

Mary read the scroll. "God _____ the world."

"You're getting closer to solving the secret," said Jesus.

"Do you know what it is?" asked Mary.

"Yes," said Jesus. He smiled. "Who do you think wrote the scrolls?"

Mary's eyes got as big as globes. "When did you write them?"

"A long, long time ago," said Jesus.

"You sure have been around a long time," said Peter.

"I always have been, and I always will be," said Jesus. "My Father and I love this world so much that he sent me to rescue it."

Peter felt a pain in his leg. "Can you help me?"

"What can I do for you?" asked Jesus.

"Can you please heal the cut on my leg?" asked Peter.

Jesus bent down and looked deep into Peter's eyes. "Do you believe in me?"

"Yes," said Peter. "I believe!"

Jesus laid his hand on Peter's head. Peter felt something warm flow from the top of his head and down through his body like a wave of love and energy. He felt a tingle in his leg, and the pain went away.

"Take off the bandage," said Jesus.

Peter peeled off the bandage. The cut was healed! The only thing left was a small scar.

"I left the scar so you will remember," said Jesus.

"Don't worry," said Peter. "I will never forget."

9

Multiplying Miracles

Peter ran in a circle and jumped up and down. "My leg feels great!"

"Thank you for healing Peter's leg," said Mary. "I have so many questions for you."

Jesus smiled. "I know you do. You'll find the answers in the scrolls."

Jesus pointed to the crowd. "Follow me. I have some good news to tell everyone."

Peter, Mary, and Hank followed Jesus. He climbed on top of a rock. A huge crowd of men, women, and children covered the hillside.

Peter and Mary sat on a large rock with Simon and Andrew. Hank lay on the ground at Peter's feet.

"Blessed are you who are poor," said Jesus. "You will have the Kingdom of God. Blessed are you who are hungry. You will be filled."

"Good," said Peter. "Because I'm starting to get hungry."

"*Shhhh*," said Mary.

"Blessed are you who are sad," said Jesus. He turned to a woman crying beside the rock. "The time is coming when you will laugh with joy." The woman smiled.

"Love your enemies," said Jesus. "Do good things and pray for anyone who hates you."

"Ruff!" barked Hank.

"That means you have to stop chasing squirrels, Hank," said Peter.

"Treat others the same way you want to be treated," said Jesus.

"Woof! Woof!" Hank jumped up and wagged his tail.

"No, Hank," whispered Peter. "Jesus doesn't have a treat for you."

"Do not judge people around you," said Jesus. "So that you will not be judged. Forgive everyone and you will be forgiven."

"I forgive you for dragging me through the

water and cutting my leg," Peter said to Mary.

"But it wasn't my fault!" said Mary.

"Whatever you say," said Peter. "I still forgive you."

"Give to others," said Jesus, "and God will give back to you even more than you gave."

"Mary, you need to remember that the next time I ask to borrow something," whispered Peter.

"The person who hears my words and follows them is like a man who builds his house on a strong foundation," said Jesus. "When a mighty storm comes and floodwaters hit his house, it stands! But the person who hears my words and doesn't do them is like a man who builds his house on the sand. When the storm comes, the house will be destroyed!"

The sun began to set behind the distant hills.

"Jesus," said Simon. "I don't mean to interrupt, but it's getting late and the people are hungry."

"Well, let's feed them," said Jesus.

"We don't have any food," said James.

"All this talk about food is making me hungry," said Peter. He opened the leather bag and pulled out the bread and fish he had saved.

Simon walked over to Peter.

"Will you share your food with the crowd, Peter?" asked Simon.

Peter looked down at his food. Mary nudged him and gave him *the look*.

"I guess so." He passed the food to Simon.

Andrew looked around at the thousands of people on the hillside. "Simon, that's not enough to feed this huge crowd."

"Tell everyone to sit down," said Jesus. He looked over at Peter and smiled.

The disciples moved through the crowd, instructing everyone to sit.

"What do we do now?" asked Thomas. "There is no way we can feed this crowd with five loaves of bread and two small fish."

"I'd say there are at least five thousand men," said Matthew. "That's not even counting the women and children."

Everyone seemed to be waiting to see what Jesus would do. Jesus took the bread and held it up to the sky. He said a prayer of thanks and broke the loaf of bread. He started handing bread to the disciples. They filled basket after basket. Then the disciples passed out bread to the crowd. Again and again the disciples came back to Jesus for more, and again and again he filled their baskets.

"Jesus fed everyone! I didn't realize I had so much bread," said Peter.

"You didn't," said Mary. "Jesus is multiplying the bread."

"I didn't know he was doing math," said Peter.

"It's not math!" said Mary. "It's a miracle!"

Then Jesus picked up the fish, said another prayer, and started handing it out. Just like the bread, the fish never ran out, and everyone was fed. Peter even saw the disciples gathering up leftovers! Everyone was talking about the incredible thing Jesus had done.

"Look," said Mary.

"I know," said Peter. "Isn't it amazing how many people are eating my fish?"

"Not that," said Mary. "It's the Pharisee with the golden staff! Quick, duck!"

Peter and Mary ducked behind a rock.

"I think he saw us," said Mary. "Can you see what he's doing?"

Peter peeked around the rock. "He's talking to a group of temple guards. He's pointing over here!"

"The thieves you're looking for are over there!" shouted the Pharisee. "Get them!"

10

DOG OVERBOARD!

Peter turned to run and bumped into Simon. "The temple guards are chasing us! What should we do?"

"Go down to my boat and hide," said Simon. "Wait for me there. Go quickly!"

Peter, Mary, and Hank ran across the hillside. They darted, ducked, and dashed through the crowd. Hank ran past them and headed down the hill toward the disciple's boat.

The sun dropped lower in the sky as they raced down the hill.

"Hurry!" shouted Peter. "We have to make it to the boat before they get us."

Hank jumped into the boat and barked.

"Be quiet, Hank," whispered Mary. "We don't want them to find us."

Peter threw the leather bag into the boat and helped Mary climb in. Then he grabbed the bow of the boat and pulled himself in. They ducked and hid as the boat bobbed in the water.

"Are they coming?" whispered Mary.

Peter peeked over the side. "It's hard to see with the sun going down, but I think we lost them."

"What do we do now?" said Mary.

"Wait for Simon, I guess," said Peter.

They waited and waited. Peter thought about the boat they'd seen in Great-Uncle Solomon's barn. It gave him an idea. He reached into the adventure bag and found the pocket knife. He crawled to the front of the boat and started carving.

"What are you doing?" said Mary. "This isn't our boat."

Peter looked up. "I'm almost done."

"Doing what?" said Mary.

"I'll explain later," said Peter.

"Grrrr." Hank made a low growl.

Mary's eyes widened. "Did you hear that?"

Peter closed his eyes and listened. He heard footsteps coming down the hill. Lots of footsteps. Then he heard men's voices. He looked over at Mary. She was trembling.

They laid still and quiet on the deck of the boat. Peter's heart pounded. He saw someone's face peer over the side of the boat.

Peter let out a big sigh of relief. It was Simon. He climbed in with the other disciples.

"I'm glad you three are safe," said Simon.

"Me too," said Mary. "That was close."

"Too close," said Peter.

"So," said Simon. "Are you ready to tell me why temple guards are chasing you?"

Peter and Mary looked at each other and shook their heads.

Simon nodded. "Your secret is safe with us. Jesus told us to meet him on the other side of the Sea of Galilee. Would you like to come?"

Peter and Mary looked at each other. A big grin spread across Mary's face.

"We'd love to!" said Peter.

"Good. Then let's get out of here," said Simon. The disciples picked up the oars and started rowing. The boat eased away from shore and headed through the dark water.

"Raise the sail!" shouted Simon.

The disciples grabbed ropes and pulled. Peter joined them. The wind filled the sail, and the boat picked up speed.

The sky grew darker and darker. Thick black

clouds rolled in and covered the moon. The wind blew harder. The boat sped faster and faster through the water.

Peter wiped raindrops from his forehead. "I hope this storm doesn't get too bad!"

But it did. The wind howled. The waves rolled and the boat rocked. Peter tripped and rolled across the deck. The leather bag fell off his shoulder and slid to the edge of the boat.

"Hank!" shouted Peter. "Get the bag."

"Ruff! Ruff!" Hank ran across the boat.

Just then a huge wave crashed into the side of the boat, tipping it sideways and almost turning it over. Peter was thrown across the boat. He grabbed the mast to steady himself. Mary held onto the side of the boat. The disciples shouted to each other as they tried to keep rowing. Some prayed for God to stop the storm.

The boat rocked and the leather bag bounced

into the air. Peter watched as it splashed into the water. Hank ran to the edge of the boat.

"Hank, no!" shouted Peter.

It was too late. Hank jumped out of the boat. Peter stared down into the dark water. Hank was struggling against the crashing waves as he grabbed the bag.

"Help!" shouted Peter. "Dog overboard!"

Simon ran to his side. "Grab the fishing net!"

Mary and Andrew brought the net over. Simon hurled the net toward Hank.

"You got him!" said Peter. "Pull him in!"

Everyone grabbed the nets and pulled. Hank splashed back on board with the bag in his mouth.

Peter untangled Hank from the net.

Mary opened the bag. "Everything is safe."

"That bag must be very important," said Simon.

"You have no idea," said Peter. "Thanks for your help."

"We're not out of danger yet!" said Thomas. "I think we're about to sink!"

Peter looked down. Water was filling the boat.

Andrew shouted and pointed behind the boat. "I think I see a ghost!"

11

Miracles by the Sea

The disciples ran to the other side of the boat. *They look really scared,* Peter thought. He stared into the dark and stormy night.

Waves crashed and water splashed his face. Peter wiped his eyes and tried to focus. Finally, he saw something. "I don't think it's a ghost."

"What is it?" said Mary.

"Don't be afraid!" said a voice from across the raging sea. "I am here!"

"It's Jesus!" said Peter.

"Lord, if it's you," shouted Simon, "tell me to come to you on the water."

"Yes!" said Jesus. "Come to me."

Peter looked at the dark, crashing waves and then looked at Simon. "You're braver than I am."

Simon climbed onto the edge of the boat, took a deep breath, and jumped. His feet landed on top of the water.

"He's not sinking!" said Andrew.

Simon took one step—then another. He was walking on the water toward Jesus!

A strong wave crashed into Simon's side. He took his eyes off Jesus and looked down at the rough sea. Immediately Simon began to sink.

Simon reached out his hand and said, "Lord, save me!"

Jesus reached down and pulled Simon from the raging sea. "You have such little faith," he said. "Why didn't you trust me?"

Jesus helped Simon climb back into the boat, then he came aboard. Jesus lifted his hands toward the dark sky. The wind stopped. The waves calmed. And the boat became still.

Peter could hardly believe what he had just seen. He looked at Mary and the wide-eyed disciples. They seemed as shocked as he was.

"You really are the Son of God!" said Thomas.

"Now, let's get to the

shore," said Jesus. And just like that—they were landing on the shore.

Hank jumped out of the boat first. Peter and Mary hopped out. It was nice to be on land again.

The sun was rising above the hills. There was a man running down the hill toward the boat. He looked tired and his clothes were dirty.

The man ran up and fell at Jesus' feet.

Jesus grabbed the man's hands and pulled him to his feet. "What can I do for you?"

The man leaned over to catch his breath. "I came all the way from Bethany. I have a message from Martha and her sister Mary." He took another deep breath.

"Yes," said Jesus. "I know them well."

"Their brother, Lazarus, the one you love, is sick!" the man said.

Simon ran up to Jesus. "If Lazarus is sick, we must go! You can heal him."

Jesus spoke gently to Simon. "This sickness won't end in death. He is sick so you can see how great God is, and so that more people can know I am the Son of God."

"Should we leave now? It's a long journey to Bethany," said Simon.

Jesus looked at a crowd of people coming down the hill toward them. "No," he said. "We have more work to do here."

"Why isn't Jesus going to help his friend?" Peter whispered to Mary.

"I don't know," she said. "We have to trust him."

Peter, Mary, and Hank spent that day and the next with the disciples, following Jesus as he helped people around the Sea of Galilee. At the end of the second day, they all set up camp beside the sea. Under the light of the moon, Peter took out his adventure journal and wrote.

Day 4

I didn't have time to write yesterday.
Jesus is helping so many people
around the Sea of Galilee. He healed
one man who was covered in oozing
sores. Everyone was afraid to get
near him, but Jesus just walked up
and touched him. The man's skin
cleared up right in front of me. The
people were excited and gave the
man hugs. He was pretty happy! Then
we saw this blind man. Jesus spit in
the dirt and made some mud and
smeared it on the man's eyes. Mary
thought it was gross. But when the
man washed it off, he could see! I
can't believe we are getting to spend
so much time with Jesus and the
disciples!

Day 5

Jesus healed more people today. One lady just touched his robe, and she wasn't sick anymore. Jesus also told stories about a Good Samaritan, a Prodigal Son, and a lost sheep. The stories were kind of confusing, but Jesus told us what they meant. They're usually about loving everyone and believing and trusting in God. I'm learning so much from Jesus, but I'm starting to get nervous about solving the secret of the scroll. If we don't solve it in two days, we will be stuck here forever, and we'll never get to see our parents or Great-Uncle Solomon again.

Peter put his adventure journal away and fell asleep under the starry sky.

12

The Plot Thickens

Peter woke the next morning and looked over at Mary. She stretched and stood up. Hank wagged his tail and licked Peter's hand.

"Good morning," said Jesus. He was standing in the middle of the camp. "I have something to tell you all."

Peter and Mary joined the disciples as they gathered around Jesus.

"It is time to go to Bethany," said Jesus. "Our friend Lazarus has fallen asleep, and I'm going to wake him up."

Simon wrinkled his eyebrows. "If Lazarus is asleep, won't he just wake up on his own?"

Jesus took a deep breath. "Lazarus is dead."

Peter heard gasps and cries from the disciples.

Jesus spoke softly, "I am glad that I was not there, because now you will really believe."

Peter looked around. The disciples' heads hung low, and their shoulders drooped. Peter saw tears on Simon's cheeks.

"Let's go see Lazarus," said Jesus.

The disciples packed up camp, and Peter grabbed the adventure bag. They joined Jesus and the disciples on the two-day journey along the Jordan River. It was a long, rough, and hot trip. Peter wished they had the horses. It would have been much easier.

Toward the end of the second day, Jesus said, "We're almost there."

Peter kicked a small rock along the dirt path.

Hank chased it and brought it back. Soon Peter saw the Temple gleaming in the sunlight. He didn't know they were going to be so close to Jerusalem and the Temple. He worried about the Pharisees and the temple guards. They felt too close.

"*Woof!*" Hank barked at a group of women coming toward them on the road. One fell in the dirt at Jesus' feet. There were tears running through the dust on her face.

"Lord, if you had been here," she cried, "my brother wouldn't have died."

Jesus knelt down and held the woman's hand. "Your brother will rise again." He stood and lifted her up. "I am the Resurrection and the Life. Whoever believes in me, even if they die, will live forever. Do you believe this?"

"Yes," she said. "I believe you are the Son of God."

Jesus looked at her tear-streaked face. Peter

saw Jesus' chest heave up and down. Tears rolled down Jesus' face.

Jesus must have really loved Lazarus, Peter thought. He felt tears welling up in his own eyes. Mary was crying too. Hank's ears were low, and his tail wasn't wagging at all.

"Where did you put Lazarus?" asked Jesus.

"Come and see," said one of the women.

Jesus wiped tears from his cheek and followed her.

Peter, Mary, and Hank walked close behind with the other women and the disciples. The

dusty path led them to a hill. Peter saw several huge round stones resting against the hillside.

"What are those?" said Peter.

"We're in a cemetery," whispered Mary. "They bury people in caves and roll big stones in front of the entrances."

Peter looked around at all the people who were crying. He felt sad and uncomfortable. He didn't like funerals or cemeteries.

Jesus walked toward one of the large stones. "Roll away the stone," he said.

Martha looked worried. "But Jesus, Lazarus has been dead for four days and he will stink!"

Peter imagined what Lazarus's body might look like and a chill ran though his body.

Jesus turned to Martha. "Didn't I tell you that if you believe, you will see amazing miracles from God?"

Martha nodded and some people rolled the

stone away. Jesus walked closer to the dark, open space. Peter and Mary joined the crowd as it gathered behind him. Everyone was silent.

Jesus looked up to the sky and prayed. "Father, thank you for listening to me. I say this so that the people standing around me will believe."

Jesus took another step toward the grave. "Lazarus, come out!" he shouted.

His voice was so loud and powerful that it reminded Peter of the lion's roar. Peter heard Jesus' voice echo back from the grave.

No one took their eyes off the open grave. Suddenly Peter heard a soft shuffling. Then someone wrapped in white cloth walked out of the grave. Peter thought he looked like a mummy.

"Unwrap him!" said Jesus. "And let him go!"

Martha and her sister ran forward and

unwrapped Lazarus' head. Lazarus took a deep breath and smiled.

"He's alive!" shouted Martha.

I can hardly believe my eyes, thought Peter. He heard shouts of joy and amazement as the crowd watched Lazarus hug his sisters. But he saw one person at the back of the crowd who wasn't happy.

Peter grabbed Mary's hand and pulled her behind the rock that had been rolled away.

"What are you doing?" said Mary.

"Look who's here." Peter pointed through the crowd at the Pharisee with the golden staff.

Hank growled. Peter held him back as the group of Pharisees walked closer to their hiding place.

"We have to end this!" snarled the Pharisee with the golden staff.

"I agree," said another Pharisee. "He has become far too powerful. The people would follow him anywhere."

"What should we do?" said a third Pharisee.

"It's time to make a plan with the High Priest," answered the Pharisee with the staff. "We must go to the Temple at once!"

The Pharisees started walking down the path toward Jerusalem.

"We have to follow them," said Peter, "and find out their plan."

Mary twisted her hair. "What if we get caught? Today is our last day to solve the secret of the scroll. Maybe we should stay here and try to figure it out."

Peter had forgotten that it was the last day to solve the scroll, but he knew they needed to go. "We have to trust in God. He'll help us."

Mary nodded her head. "You're right."

"Let's go!"

13

Not This Time

Peter, Mary, and Hank moved through the crowd as they made their way to the path.

"Where do you think you're going?" said a voice.

"*Grrrr!*" Hank growled at someone behind them.

Peter turned and saw Judas.

"We can't tell you," said Mary. "But we'll be back soon."

"You two are full of secrets," said Judas. "Do you want me to keep your bag safe while you're gone?"

Peter held the adventure bag tight by his side. "No thanks. I'll take care of it."

Judas lowered his eyebrows. "Be careful. You never know who you can trust."

Peter felt a lump in his throat. "We will," he said, slowly backing away.

They turned and ran to the path. They could see the Pharisees ahead of them. They followed, careful to stay back far enough so the Pharisees wouldn't see them.

They followed the Pharisees down the dusty trail. It led over a tall hill covered in olive trees and then down into a deep valley filled with large rocks and dry shrubs.

"There's the Temple!" said Mary.

Up ahead, Peter saw the golden roof of the Temple poking above the tall stone wall surrounding Jerusalem. He watched the Pharisees enter a gate at the base of the wall.

Peter, Mary, and Hank carefully followed the Pharisees through the gate, up some stairs, through another gate, and into the Temple courtyard. The sun was setting behind the Temple. The time to solve the secret of the scroll was running out.

"They're stopping," said Mary.

"Hide," said Peter. "Behind these plants."

Peter peeked around the plants. He saw the Pharisees enter a door on the side of the Temple. "I don't think they saw us," he said.

A few other men in fancy robes entered the same door. Peter waited until they had all entered the Temple.

"The coast is clear," he said.

They snuck through the door and found themselves in a large room with columns all around it. They hid behind a large column in the back corner of the room.

"What are they doing?" asked Mary.

Peter peeked around the column. "Everyone's standing in front of an old man," he whispered. "He's wearing a colorful robe with huge jewels on it."

"He must be the High Priest," said Mary.

Peter ducked back behind the column. "The Pharisee with the golden staff just walked up to the High Priest."

Peter and Mary listened as the Pharisee told

the High Priest and all the others about Jesus raising Lazarus from the dead.

"What should we do, Caiaphas?" said the Pharisee. "If we allow Jesus to go on this way, everyone will follow him, and the people will try to make him king!" The Pharisee's voice grew louder. "Then the Romans will come and destroy us!"

Peter heard the Pharisees arguing and shouting at each other.

"Silence!" shouted High Priest Caiaphas. He rubbed his beard. "One man must die so that the whole nation is not destroyed!"

"Yes!" shouted the Pharisee with the golden staff. "Jesus must die!"

Peter squinted. He thought he saw a smile on the Pharisee's face.

"We have to warn Jesus," whispered Peter. "Let's go."

They ran out of the Temple. Mary slid to a stop in the middle of the courtyard.

"What are you doing?" said Peter.

Mary pointed at the moon high in the sky. "We're almost out of time," she said. "We have to solve the scroll right now or we'll be stuck here!" Peter's heart pounded. He wanted to warn Jesus, but he knew Mary was right.

"Grrrr!" Hank growled.

Peter spun around and saw someone slowly walking out from the shadows of the Temple.

"Did you say something about a scroll?" asked the Pharisee with the golden staff.

Peter gripped the adventure bag and slowly backed up.

"Where do you think you're going?" said the Pharisee.

"We're going to tell Jesus about your plan!" said Peter.

"So, you heard my little plan," said the Pharisee. "It doesn't matter."

"Your plan won't work!" said Mary.

The Pharisee slammed his golden staff on the ground. "You kids have caused me trouble in the past," he snarled. "But not this time!"

Peter could see rage in the Pharisee's eyes. They looked so familiar.

"I will kill God's Son!" the Pharisee shouted. "Then the Earth and all its people will be mine!"

"Satan!" said Mary. "We should have known it was you!"

"It's too late! You can't stop my plan now!"

"God can!" said Peter. "He always does."

The Pharisee laughed. "Not this time. Guards!"

Hank barked as several guards ran out of the Temple.

"I found your little thieves!" said the Pharisee.

The guards surrounded Peter, Mary, and Hank.

The Pharisee pointed his golden staff at Peter. "You will find your scroll in his bag!"

One guard grabbed Peter's arms. He struggled while the guard who had caught them in the library reached into the bag and pulled out the scroll.

Mary did a spinning kick through the air, but the guard moved the scroll just before she could kick it out of his hand.

"Not this time," said the guard.

Peter broke free and lunged for the scroll.

The guard pulled out his sword. "Stay back!"

"Woof! Woof!" Hank stepped in front of Peter and Mary.

"Give us back our scroll!" said Peter.

"Everyone, calm down!" said the Pharisee. "Why don't we see what's written on the scroll?"

"No!" said Mary. "You can't."

"We'll see about that," said the Pharisee. "What does it say?"

The guard unrolled the scroll and squinted as he tried to read it in the moonlight. "I can't read it," he said.

"You're worthless!" shouted the Pharisee.

The guard lowered his head and his shoulders slumped.

"Give it to me!" said the Pharisee.

The guard put away his sword and tossed the scroll to the Pharisee.

"Fetch!" Peter shouted to Hank.

Hank jumped in the air and caught the scroll.

"You can't do anything right!" said the Pharisee. "No wonder God doesn't love lowly people like you."

"Don't listen to him," said Peter. "God loves you! He doesn't just love Pharisees and powerful people. God loves everyone!"

The scroll vibrated in Hank's mouth.

"Give me that scroll!" snarled the Pharisee. He swung his golden staff.

Hank jumped over the staff and ran to Peter.

"Good boy!" said Peter. He unrolled the scroll. The second word glowed and transformed into the word: LOVES.

"Watch out!" shouted Mary.

Peter looked up and saw the Pharisee and the guards rushing at him.

"Read the scroll!" said Mary.

Peter looked down and read, "GOD LOVES THE WORLD!"

The ground started shaking, and everything around them began to spin. Peter saw the golden staff swinging toward him. He closed his eyes and ducked.

Suddenly, everything was still and quiet. Peter opened his eyes. They were safe in Great-Uncle Solomon's library.

"That was close!" said Mary.

Peter took a deep breath. "You're not kidding," he said, looking down at the scroll. The red wax seal melted and transformed into a golden medallion.

Peter rubbed his finger across the heart imprinted on the medallion. "God does love the world."

Mary smiled. "Yes, he does," she said. "Let's go tell Great-Uncle Solomon about our adventure."

They ran to the barn and found him working on the boat. Mary told him about seeing Jesus again and meeting Simon and the disciples. Peter showed his scar and explained how Jesus healed him and raised Lazarus from the dead. Then Mary told Great-Uncle Solomon about the plan to kill Jesus.

"We need to get back to warn him," said Peter.

"You'll have to wait for the lion's roar," said Great-Uncle Solomon.

Peter nodded. Then he remembered something. "Oh yeah," he said. "I have to check something!" He ran over to the boat and looked inside. "It's there!"

Great-Uncle Solomon leaned into the boat. "What's there?"

Peter pointed at the letters PT carved into the ancient wood. "My initials," he said. "I carved them in the boat before Jesus rescued us at sea because I thought it might be the same boat you had in your barn."

Great-Uncle Solomon jumped excitedly. "It's the boat!" he said. "I knew it was the boat!"

Peter stared at the gold medallion in the palm of his hand.

He couldn't wait to hear the lion roar again.

Do you want to read more
about the events in this story?

The people, places, and events in *Miracles by the Sea* are drawn from the stories in the Bible. You can read more about them in the following passages in the Bible.

Mark 2:1–12 tells the story of Jesus healing the paralyzed man lowered through the roof.
Matthew 5–7 is where you will find Jesus teaching on the mountain.
John 6:1–15 tells about Jesus feeding the five thousand.
Matthew 14:22–33 tells the exciting story of Jesus walking on the water.
John 11:1–44 tells the story of Jesus raising Lazarus from the dead.

CATCH ALL
PETER AND MARY'S
ADVENTURES!

In *The Beginning*, Peter, Mary, and Hank witness the Creation of the earth while battling a sneaky snake.

In *Race to the Ark*, the trio must rush to help Noah finish the ark before the coming flood.

In *The Great Escape*, Peter, Mary, and Hank journey to Egypt and see the devastation of the plagues.

In *Journey to Jericho*, the trio lands in Jericho as the Israelites prepare to enter the Promised Land.

In *The Shepherd's Stone*, Peter, Mary, and Hank accompany David as he prepares to fight Goliath.

In *The Lion's Roar*, the trio arrive in Babylon and uncover a plot to get Daniel thrown in the lions' den.

In *The King Is Born*, Peter, Mary, and Hank visit Bethlehem at the time of Jesus' birth.

ABOUT THE AUTHOR

 Mike Thomas grew up in Florida playing sports and riding his bike to the library and the arcade. He graduated from Liberty University, where he earned a bachelor's degree in Bible Studies.

When his son Peter was nine years old, Mike went searching for books that would teach Peter about the Bible in a fun and imaginative way. Finding none, he decided to write his own series. In The Secret of the Hidden Scrolls, Mike combines biblical accuracy with adventure, imagination, and characters who are dear to his heart. The main characters are named after Mike's son Peter, his niece Mary, and his dog, Hank.

Mike lives in Tennessee with his wife, Lori; two sons, Payton and Peter; and Hank.

For more information about the author and the series, visit www.secretofthehiddenscrolls.com.